Double Trouble

Double Trouble

Joanne Levy

ORCA BOOK PUBLISHERS

Library and Archives Canada Cataloguing in Publication

Title: Double trouble / Joanne Levy.
Names: Levy, Joanne, author.
Series: Orca currents.

Description: Series statement: Orca currents

Identifiers: Canadiana (print) 20190069643 | Canadiana (ebook) 20190069651 | ISBN 9781459821330 (softcover) | ISBN 9781459821347 (PDF) | ISBN 9781459821354 (EPUB)

Classification: LCC PS8623.E9592 D68 2019 | DDC jc813/.6—dc23

Library of Congress Control Number: 2019934032
Simultaneously published in Canada and the United States in 2019

Summary: In this high-interest novel for middle readers, twelve-year-old Victoria pretends she has an identical twin sister.

Orca Book Publishers is committed to reducing the consumption of nonrenewable resources in the making of our books. We make every effort to use materials that support a sustainable future.

Orca Book Publishers gratefully acknowledges the support for its publishing programs provided by the following agencies: the Government of Canada, the Canada Council for the Arts and the Province of British Columbia through the BC Arts Council and the Book Publishing Tax Credit.

Edited by Tanya Trafford
Cover artwork by Stocksy.com/Gillian Vann
Author photo by Tania Garshowitz

ORCA BOOK PUBLISHERS
orcabook.com

Printed and bound in Canada.

22 21 20 19 • 4 3 2 1

Chapter One

“So what’s on the harvest menu for today?” asked Bubby, my grandmother, from the front seat. We were driving home from synagogue.

I was picking at a scab on my thumb. When I looked up, I saw she was smiling at me.

“Tomatoes,” I said. She was asking what was ready for picking in my organic garden. "Maybe some lettuce and broccoli." I hate broccoli. I planted it because she likes it. I hoped she was prepared to eat a lot of it, because it was growing like crazy.

"Make sure you take off your dress before you start playing in the dirt," my dad said. He was looking at me in the rearview mirror. He called it "playing in the dirt," but I knew he was proud that I'd created the garden and tended to it myself.

I looked back down at my lap and smoothed my hands over the shiny green fabric of my dress. I hated it—because I hate *all* dresses. At least I had been allowed to pick the color of this one when Bubby had taken me shopping after we'd realized I'd outgrown all my fancy synagogue clothes. It reminded me of leaves. "Yes, Dad," I replied. I might have rolled my eyes too.

"Your grandmother paid a lot for that outfit. I'd like to see you get some more wear out of it."

Ugh, no thanks. "Yes, Dad," I said. Again.

"And you don't need to be getting it dirty."

"*Okay*! I get it, Dad!"

Bubby winked and then turned around to face the road. "That was a lovely service at synagogue," she said. "Maxa did a great job with her Torah portion."

She really had. I hoped I could do half as well at my bat mitzvah. "She's been practicing for months," I said.

"Just like you will when it's your turn," Dad said. He looked at me again in the mirror. "Your lessons start in the fall."

Like he needed to remind me. I had been looking forward to it when I was going to be doing bat mitzvah classes with my best friend, Anna. But Anna's family had suddenly moved away when her mom had gotten a new job. Now I was stuck going to bat mitzvah class by myself. I'd be lucky if I ever got to see Anna again. She'd promised to invite me to her family's Purim masquerade party, but that was months from now.

This summer had been *so* lonely. I'd always wished for brothers and sisters, but never so much as this year. At least I had my garden to keep me busy. Someday I was going to be a food scientist and solve the world's food-shortage problem.

But for now I just grew what I could in our backyard garden. Most of it we ate fresh. Some Bubby preserved in jars for the winter, like pickles and tomatoes.

I used to give some to Anna and her family too. But since she moved, I have been taking extras to our neighbors, like

Ms. Simon and her five-year-old twin daughters, Maisey and Daisy. They live across the street. I didn't know them very well since they'd just moved in at the beginning of the summer. But Ms. Simon seemed nice and had even asked me for some advice on her little herb garden.

I also took some over to the Patels—the old couple who live next door.

Everyone appreciated my veggies, but it isn't the same as sharing with my bestie. The Patels like broccoli though.

As soon we pulled into the driveway, I jumped out of the car. I couldn't wait to change my clothes and get to work in the garden. I was partway up the porch stairs when I noticed the Patels' big burgundy car pulling into their driveway. There was someone in the back seat.

A young girl—about my age—stepped out of the car. She had dark skin like Mr. and Mrs. Patel. Her long black hair was tied back in a high ponytail.

"Hello, Mr. and Mrs. Patel," I called over to them. I figured that was the best way to find out who this girl was.

Mr. Patel smiled and waved. "Oh! Hello, Victoria."

"Come meet our granddaughter," Mrs. Patel added, waving me over. "She's here for a visit!"

I knew the Patels had grandkids, but they lived so far away that I'd never met them. I walked over, feeling a little bit nervous.

"Hello," I said.

"Nice to meet you, Victoria," the girl said with a big smile. "My name is Jasvitha, but my friends call me Jazzy."

"Jazzy's a cool name," I said, relaxing a bit. She already seemed nice.

"We'll let you girls get to know each other," Mrs. Patel said as she reached into the trunk and pulled out two shopping bags. Mr. Patel took a large suitcase out of the back seat. "But not too long, Jasvitha," she added. "We have groceries to put away."

"Yes, Dida." Jazzy nodded and then turned back to me. "I'm staying with them until Labor Day," she said.

Labor Day! That was two whole weeks away. My brain started whirling. I was already getting really excited about having someone to hang out with for the last days of summer.

"Oh, really?" I asked, trying to play it cool.

She nodded. "My parents are in Australia looking for a house. My dad just got a new job there, so we're moving. I'm here for a visit with Dadu and Dida—my grandparents—because it will be a long time before I see them again. They won't fly all that way, so..."

I couldn't imagine moving a half a world away from Bubby. I would hate it if she lived even across town. But my grandmother is like a mom to me. My mom died when I was very young.

"Wow," I said. "Australia is far."

Jazzy shrugged. Then she looked me up and down, from my shoes to my dress. "I *love* your outfit," she blurted.

I looked down at my dress. Even though I hated it, I knew I looked good in it. Especially paired with the glittery silver shoes (which I also hated) and my fancy hairdo with hairspray that itched (Bubby had insisted).

"Thanks," I said. I was going to talk about how much I hated dresses, but I could tell that Jazzy loved it. She even reached out to touch the fabric on the sleeve.

"Is that silk?" she asked.

I shrugged. "No idea."

"I bet it's silk," she said with a nod. "It's stunning. You have such great taste."

"That's me, all about fashion," I said.

"It really shows," she said. She didn't seem to notice I was being sarcastic. I didn't want to make her feel bad, so I didn't say anything else.

"Jasvitha!" Mr. Patel hollered from their side door. "You can play later. Come put your things away. Then it's time for lunch."

"Yes, Dadu!" Jazzy yelled over her shoulder. "I'd better go," she said to me. "But I'll see you later, okay?"

"Yes," I said. "That would be cool."

Then she leaned in and gave me a surprise hug. "I'm only here for two weeks," she said, "but I already know we're going to be best friends."

Perfect. A new best friend was exactly what I needed.

Chapter Two

I changed out of that uncomfortable dress, had some lunch and went out to my garden. I kept an eye on the Patels' backyard. Maybe I was hoping to see Jazzy.

No, I was *definitely* hoping to see Jazzy. Since we were going to be best friends and all. May as well get started on that, I figured.

But she didn't come out of the house. I didn't want to interrupt whatever she was doing inside, so I focused on picking sugar snap peas. I wondered if Jazzy liked peas. They'd been Anna's favorite, which was why I had planted them in the first place.

Now I saved them for Maisey and Daisy—the cute twins across the street. They liked popping the little peas out of their pods and straight into their mouths. I'd take some over to them later.

Soon I was done the day's harvest—peas, tomatoes and the dreaded broccoli. Jazzy still hadn't come out. I started pulling some weeds.

Still no Jazzy.

Maybe she was watching a movie or helping prepare dinner. I tried not to let my imagination come up with a zillion reasons why she wasn't coming to see me—her soon-to-be new best friend. Except it was all I could think about.

I went into the house and traded the basket of fresh vegetables for the compost bin we keep under the counter. I took it outside.

Still no Jazzy.

I took the compost into the shed and pulled the lid off my worm bin.

Yes, I said worm bin. As in real, live worms. Red wigglers, to be precise. I pulled back the newspaper bedding and dug a hole for the scraps. Banana peels, strawberry tops, chopped-up broccoli stalks.

I knew my worms would eat everything, even the vegetables *I* didn't like. I fed them our kitchen scraps, and they made organic fertilizer. We have a great relationship that way. Not quite a friendship. But as I thought about the hug I'd received from the Patels' granddaughter, I hoped that now I'd have a *real* friend. With arms and everything.

I looked out the dirty window of the shed.

Finally! There she was! I watched her open the sliding glass door at the back of the house and head toward my yard. She had a big smile on her face. One that matched mine.

I quickly put the rest of the scraps into the bin, covered them up and closed the lid. I stepped out of the shed and called out a loud, "Hi!"

Jazzy looked at me, her smile disappearing. "Oh, hi there." She glanced over toward the house. "I'm looking for Victoria."

"Huh?" I asked. Because, uh, *I* am Victoria.

"I met her earlier," Jazzy said. "She was wearing a stunning green dress. Elegant hair, sparkly shoes?"

She was looking at me like we'd never met. I was starting to think maybe she was a little nuts.

Then I looked down at myself. Ratty old T-shirt and jeans, hands covered in worm and food-scrap muck. My hair shoved under a baseball cap, and Crocs caked with mud. Hardly elegant.

"Oh, I…"

"Ugh, what is that all over your hands?" Jazzy asked with a frown.

I put my arms behind my back, even though it was too late to hide them. "Worm castings."

Her frown went from disgust to confusion. "What are *worm castings*?"

"Worm poop," I said, though very quietly, like maybe she wouldn't hear.

"WORM POOP?!" Nope, nothing wrong with her hearing. "Like, poop from actual *worms*?"

I nodded. I was thinking how nice it would have been to have a new best friend. Not much chance of that now.

"Worm. Poop." She gagged. "That is *disgusting*."

"It's not as gross as it sounds," I said a bit helplessly. "It's for my garden." I waved toward my vegetable beds.

"Poop. You put worm poop in your garden."

I was getting annoyed that she kept repeating herself. But what could I do? I just nodded.

"Gross."

I just stood there, silent.

"Anyway," she said, crossing her arms. Her shirt had a big daisy on the front of it. "I'm here to see Vicky. Is she around? We were going to hang out."

So...wait. Jazzy *still* didn't recognize me as the girl she'd met earlier? *And* she was calling *that girl* Vicky?

As Jazzy stared at me like I was simple, I stared at her shirt. It made me think of Daisy across the street.

I suddenly had an idea. One that might save the best-friend thing. "Oh, right,"

I said quickly. "Vicky is inside having a nap. I'm her twin sister, Tori."

Okay, so I didn't say that it was a *good* idea.

Chapter Three

As soon as Jazzy left, I speed-walked through the backyard. Once I was inside, I kicked my Crocs off onto the mat at the back door.

My dad was standing in the middle of the kitchen. He'd changed out of his good suit and into jeans. His keys were in his hand.

"C'mon," he said. "I'm heading to the hardware store."

"Can't, Dad," I said, going around him. "Busy."

"Too busy to go to the hardware store?" he asked. His eyebrows were raised high. "You love the hardware store!"

That was true. And a part of me did want to go with him. But today I had a new friend to impress. And she wasn't going to be impressed by my growing collection of garden tools.

"Sorry, Dad. No time."

I hurried to the bathroom. I wanted to take a quick shower. But when I saw the door was closed, I sighed and went to my room. I looked in my closet for some clothes I thought Jazzy would think were fashionable.

It didn't take long to realize I had nothing that *anyone* would consider fashionable.

"That one dress is all I have that fits," I said to my closet. "And I can't go hang out with Jazzy in that."

My grandmother was always trying to get me to go shopping with her for nice clothes. I hated shopping but had agreed we could go buy some back-to-school outfits. We hadn't gotten around to it yet. It didn't really matter though, since there was no time to go before I'd be seeing Jazzy again.

I would have to figure something out. But first I needed to get clean.

I changed out of my gardening clothes and into my robe. I got to the bathroom just as my grandmother was coming out.

"I need a shower," I explained.

She nodded. "I'm off to Sandra's to play mah-jongg. See you at dinner. Maybe we'll have broccoli with beef," she said.

"Very funny," I replied.

She smirked, then gave me a kiss on the forehead and walked away.

I washed my hair twice and even used conditioner. I left the bathroom and peeked out the front window. I needed to make sure I was home alone. When I saw no cars in the driveway, I rushed into my grandmother's room.

I pulled open her closet and began to rifle through her clothes.

At the back I found a shirt she hadn't worn for a while. It was colorful and bright. I'd always thought it looked good on her. "Bingo," I said. I pulled the shirt out and took it to my room.

Once I was dressed and had combed out my long hair, I looked in the mirror and liked what I saw. "And now," I said to my reflection, "I am Vicky."

I got to the front hall and looked at the pile of shoes there. I didn't have any nice sandals. Bubby's feet were way bigger than mine, so I couldn't borrow any of hers.

I put my sparkly shoes back on. Why not? I thought.

I left the house and was about to head over to the Patels' when I stopped in my tracks. I hadn't really thought my plan through. What if Mrs. Patel answered the door and called me Tori in front of Jazzy? It was Jazzy who had assumed my nickname was Vicky.

I'd have to take the chance. I skipped up their front porch and knocked on the door.

"I'll get it!" I heard from inside. *Whew.*

And then there she was. My new best friend.

Except as I said, "Hi!" the smile seemed to fall off her face.

"What's wrong?" I asked in a quiet voice. Had she already figured out my secret?

I held my breath, waiting to get busted. But Jazzy looked me up and down. "Um, what are you *wearing*?" she asked.

I looked down at myself and then back up to her. "What do you mean?"

"Your outfit," she said, in the same way she'd said "worm poop" earlier. "It's like...I don't know, so *old lady*."

Okay. So maybe borrowing my sixty-four-year-old grandmother's shirt with the giant roses all over it wasn't my best move.

Ugh. I was already a fashion fail. Unless…

I remembered a movie I'd watched with Bubby a few weeks back. It was all about the fashion industry and the crazy clothes they made for shows. Rich people paid zillions of dollars for them *because* they were so crazy. Bubby said it was like artwork that people can wear.

Giant flowers can be artwork.

You've got this, I thought. Just act like you own the outfit.

"*Old lady*?" I said with a shake of my head. "Are you kidding? This is what they're wearing in Paris. On all the fashion driveways."

"Driveways?" Jazzy said, frowning. "Don't you mean *runways*?"

Oops! "That's what they call them in France," I said quickly. I added an eye roll and a wave of my hand. Like I *really* knew what I was talking about. "They're all about the driveways."

Jazzy's eyes went wide. "Oh. Really?"

"Of course. I know *all about* fashion. That's me. Vicky, the fashion expert."

Jazzy stared at me for a long minute while I held my breath. Then she nodded. "Right. I meant, your outfit is so *grown up*. That's what I meant before by *old lady*. It's really cool. And I think the shoes totally make the outfit. I thought they looked nice with your dress before, but they look great with your shorts too."

Whew! She seemed to be buying my story. I felt a little bad for making it all up. But it was okay if it meant we would be friends. Anyway, it was too late to turn back now.

"Your clothes are nice too," I said. I mean, I assumed they were. She looked neat and clean in a pair of black-and-white striped pants that came down to her ankles and a pink T-shirt. Nothing overly special. She probably hadn't stolen *her* grandmother's clothes to try to impress me though.

"Thanks," she said with a smile. "How about I come over to your place and you show me your closet? I could use some ideas. You obviously have lots of bold ones. Since you know all about fashion."

"Right, uh..." I said, starting to panic. If she came over to look at my closet, she'd find out it was full of sweats, overalls and ratty old T-shirts. Not to mention zero sign of my twin sister!

"How about I come look at *your* clothes?" I proposed. "Maybe I can give you some pointers. My sister's sleeping right now, and I don't want to disturb her."

Jazzy's right eyebrow shot up. "I met your sister earlier, and she said *you* were taking a nap."

"We both take a lot of naps," I explained. "And almost never at the same time."

Jazzy nodded and then said, "She was covered in worms."

"Worm *castings*," I corrected. "The worms stay in the bin."

Her eyebrow went up again. "Right."

"Not that *I'm* into worms," I assured her, making a face. "Worms are disgusting. Worm poop. *Gross*!"

"So gross," Jazzy agreed. "Anyway, come on in. I can't wait to get your opinion on my wardrobe. I don't have everything here, but I did pack my best summer stuff."

I followed her inside and kicked off my shoes. "Where are your grandparents?" I asked. I hoped I just sounded curious, but really I did not want to have to explain to *them* who Vicky was.

Jazzy waved toward the den. "In there, watching TV. Dadu is probably sleeping. They had to get up super early to pick me up from the airport."

Just then we heard a loud snore. Jazzy and I looked at each other and nearly burst out laughing.

"I flew here all by myself, you know."

"Whoa, really?" I asked as she led me toward the spare room that was now her bedroom.

"Yeah. It was a long flight, but not as long as it will be flying to Australia."

Right. Because Jazzy was only going to be here for two weeks.

Maybe that was a good thing. It was already exhausting trying to lead a double life.

Chapter Four

"Will you take me to the mall?" I asked my grandmother the next morning. We were in the kitchen, eating breakfast.

Bubby's fork clattered to her plate. "What?" she asked, looking at me in surprise.

Keeping my eyes on my food, I shrugged. "I think I need some new clothes." I used the side of my fork to cut a piece of the cheese-and-spinach omelet Dad had made. "For school. And I probably need another dress for Rosh Hashanah and Yom Kippur. Nothing fits, remember?"

"I thought I was going to have to drag you kicking and screaming to the mall," she said.

"Just go with it," my dad said over his mug of coffee.

Bubby turned toward him and snorted loudly. "I'm not arguing," she said. "I'm just wondering what brought this on."

"I don't know," I mumbled as I finished chewing. "I just want to look nice at synagogue and when the whole family comes for the high holidays."

There was a long silence. I looked up to see Bubby and Dad exchanging weird looks. I almost told them to forget it, but I did need some new clothes. Ones Jazzy wouldn't think were old-ladyish.

"Well, whatever the reason," Bubby said, leaning across the table to put her hand on my arm, "I'd be happy to take you."

After breakfast I took the used coffee grounds out to the worms. They love wet, ground-up coffee beans. Dad jokes that they'll take their coffee any way they can get it.

I was about to check on my vegetables when the back door squeaked open.

"Tori?" my grandmother called out. "Can you come in here, please?"

Uh-oh. She wasn't using her stern voice, so I didn't think I was in trouble. Something was up though. I could tell.

I brushed off my hands and went back into the house.

I washed my hands at the kitchen sink while Bubby sat down at the table.

When I turned, I finally knew what this was all about. The shirt with the big roses on it, the one that I'd worn the day before, was draped over the back of one of the kitchen chairs. I had put it in my laundry hamper and forgotten about it. I'd also forgotten that today was the day Bubby did laundry.

Whoops.

I took a deep breath. I was about to get in trouble for borrowing without asking.

"Have a seat, Tori," Bubby said. But she still didn't sound mad. Which was weird.

I dried my hands on the dish towel and sat down beside her. I was about to apologize when Bubby reached for my hand and gave it a squeeze. She was looking at me funny.

"What is going on?" I asked.

"I want to talk to you about this,"

she said, pointing at the shirt with her free hand.

"Okay..."

"I want to make sure you're all right."

Other than being totally confused? "Yes," I said. "I'm fine."

"If you want to talk about your mom, I understand."

My *mom*? "Huh?"

Bubby seemed sad. "You obviously remember that your mother bought me that shirt as a Hanukkah gift the year you were born. Wearing it probably makes you feel close to her. Or maybe sad, since the anniversary of her death is coming up."

I had to think about the date. I guessed she was right. But my mom died so long ago that it wasn't something I thought about a lot.

But it was obviously something

my grandmother thought about. "We can talk about it anytime," she said. "I understand wanting to be close to someone you've lost, Tori."

The thing was, she *didn't* understand. I didn't even remember my mother, which made me feel a bit weird and a little guilty. I was only a baby when she died, so it's not like I miss her.

But how was I supposed to explain that I'd stolen the shirt to look cool? Especially when it hadn't worked! And I certainly didn't want to tell my grandmother that the shirt my mother had bought for her was old-ladyish.

It just seemed easiest to go along with her.

I nodded. "Thank you. I hope you're not mad that I borrowed the shirt and wore it for a while."

Bubby squeezed my hand again. "I'm not mad at all. I just wanted you to know that you can always talk to me. About anything."

I nodded again, even though I couldn't really talk to her about *everything*.

I mean, seriously. I couldn't tell her I had a fake twin, could I?

Chapter Five

I was in the front hall, waiting for Bubby, when there was a knock at the front door. When I looked out the peephole, I saw Jazzy on the porch. She was smiling as she bounced from one foot to the other.

I opened the door. "Hi."

"Hey there," she said, and then frowned at me. "I...Vicky?"

I nodded and quickly pushed my hair behind my ears. I looked over my shoulder. My grandmother was still getting ready in the kitchen.

"Yes, that's me," I said. "Vicky."

Jazzy's smile got wider. "Oh, good. I wasn't sure. You and your sister look so much alike!"

"Yeah, even my family can't tell us apart!" I said.

"I bet. Anyway, I'd still love to look at your closet. Get some bold ideas."

I had never been so relieved to have plans to go shopping! "I can't," I said, pretending to be sad. "I have to go to the mall with my grandmother to get clothes for school and the Jewish high holidays. It's important to look your best when you're celebrating important religious days."

Jazzy's eyes widened. "Really? Clothes shopping?" She grabbed my arm and tugged on it really hard. "Can I pleeeeeease come with you?"

"Uhhhh...I don't know," I said as I tried to come up with an excuse why she couldn't come. "My grandmother probably won't like that..."

"Okay, kiddo, I'm ready to go," Bubby said as she came into the front hall. She smiled at Jazzy. "Oh, hi, Jasvitha. Want to come to the mall with us?"

Noooooo!

Jazzy clapped her hands excitedly. "Yes! I was just telling Vicky that I would love to go with you. Let me run next door to tell Dida."

Before I could come up with another excuse, she ran from the porch.

"Did I hear Jasvitha just call you Vicky?" Bubby asked as she slung her big purse over her shoulder and shooed me out the front door.

"Oh, ha," I said with a big laugh that I hoped didn't sound too fake. "That's just a game we're playing where we pretend there's two of me."

Bubby gave me a weird look. "Two of you?"

"Yes," I said, trying to be convincing. "The game is called Twins. It's super fun, and I think you should play along. Today I'm Vicky, so that's the only name I'll answer to."

Bubby locked the front door of our house and then turned to look at me. "All right, *Vicky*," she said with a wink.

I was relieved that she wasn't going to blow my fake story. But I did feel a bit bad that now I was lying to two people.

"Are you sure?" asked my grandmother for about the eight hundredth time. She was staring at me and looking really confused. Which made sense.

We were at the sales counter of a trendy clothing store after an afternoon of agony. I'd been trying on clothes with my new best friend. Fancy clothes. Colorful clothes. The kind of clothes I normally hated.

"Yes," I said to my grandmother, sounding very sure. In fact, the one thing I *was* sure of was that I *didn't* want all these fancy clothes.

But Jazzy had told me that teals and pinks were totally my colors. And then she had made me try on a zillion fancy and bright outfits. Outfits I had to pretend I loved and couldn't wait to wear to school and synagogue. I'd never done so much pretending in all my life. Or fake squealing.

Because Vicky was *so* into fashion.

Too bad *Tori* wasn't. In the end I told Jazzy that I also wanted to buy a couple of things for "my sister," who preferred a more simple look. I needed at least one outfit I could wear without feeling like a box of crayons.

"All right then," Bubby said as she handed her credit card to the saleslady. I felt guilty when I saw the total flash up on the cash register. I was not going to wear most of these things.

"Thirty days return or exchange on these," the salesperson said as she passed my grandmother the receipt.

Hmm. That gave me an idea. I looked around for Jazzy. She was over at the jewelry rack, looking at dangly earrings. "So these things are all returnable?" I asked quietly, so my new BFF wouldn't hear.

The woman nodded as she pushed the bag toward me. "Within thirty days."

Jazzy would be leaving for Australia in *twelve* days.

Perfect. I would just hide all the new stuff in my closet until she left. Then I could return it all.

Except what we'd bought for Tori, of course.

Chapter Six

When we got back from the mall, Jazzy went home. She had some things to do with her grandparents. I was relieved because while I liked Jazzy a lot, I was getting really tired.

Not of her, but of Vicky.

Also, shopping was exhausting. *Pretending* to like shopping was even more exhausting.

I didn't feel like a nap though. I changed into my overalls, grabbed the compost bin and went out to the shed.

When I opened the door, I was greeted by that comforting, earthy smell. I sighed in relief, already feeling better.

I knelt down and opened up my worm farm. I carefully moved aside some of the newspaper and added the kitchen scraps. As I did, I thought about the worms and how lucky they were to not have to worry about nice clothes and fitting in. All they had to worry about was eating carrot tops and potato peels. And since I brought them all the food they could eat, they probably didn't ever worry at all.

Life is simple when you're a worm.

As I put the lid back on and stood up, my phone buzzed in my pocket. I pulled it out. A text from Jazzy.

Eggplant curry 4 dinner. Then movies! Come over!

I'd barely finished reading her message before my mouth started watering. Mrs. Patel's eggplant curry was one of my very favorite dishes! Plus, movies sounded fun. Dad never wanted to watch ones I liked, and Bubby always fell asleep. The whole point of having a bestie was to do stuff like watch movies, right?

But as much as I wanted to go, I knew better. If I went over there, I would have to pretend to be Vicky. And that would be complicated around Jazzy's grandparents.

Can't. Sorry.

I hoped she knew just how sorry I was.

A second later I got a frowny face emoji. At least she didn't ask why I couldn't come.

I put my phone away and said goodbye to my worms. Then I grabbed my big, floppy hat and went out into the garden.

Since it was nearly the end of the summer, many plants were bursting with ripe vegetables. Sometimes it seemed like they appeared overnight like magic.

Like the cucumber vines. Suddenly they were loaded with little green ovals that were the perfect size for Bubby to make her famous pickles. She had been waiting for them to be ready. She was going to be so happy!

I left a few on the vines to grow bigger for salads but plucked most of them off and dropped them in my basket.

When I went into the house, Bubby was in the kitchen, making tea. "I was just going to come out and check on you," she said with a smile. "I hope you have a couple of eggplants in that basket."

"I do!" I said, showing her the basket. "Also some mini cukes for pickles."

Bubby smiled. “Between your gardening and my canning, we make a great team.”

I nodded and slid the basket onto the counter.

“These tomatoes look wonderful too.” She took two of the eggplants from the basket and handed them to me. “Take these over to Prisha.”

“What?” I said.

“Mrs. Patel. She’s making her curry tonight, and I promised her a couple of eggplants,” Bubby said.

“But…but…” What could I say? I couldn’t tell Bubby that I was scared all my lies would unravel in front of Jazzy.

Bubby tilted her head. “What’s wrong, Tori? Or is it *Vicky* today?”

Ugh! “Nothing, just…I thought we could keep them. Your eggplant parm is the best!” I put the eggplants down on the counter and rubbed my belly. “Can you make that tonight?”

Bubby tilted her head and frowned. “No, these eggplants need to go next door,” she said firmly. “I promised Prisha. Anyway, your father is bringing home Chinese tonight.”

“But I want eggplant. *Please*?”

“Victoria Sarah Adelman!”

Uh-oh. When she used all three of my names, I knew I was in trouble. Or was about to be.

Bubby’s hands were on her hips in her “angry grandmother” pose. “I don’t know what is wrong with you today, but this is not up for debate. Take those eggplants next door. Right now.”

She was staring at me with wide eyes, waiting for me to do as she said. I knew if I didn’t, I risked getting grounded.

“Fine,” I said.

“Watch your tone, young lady.”

The only thing worse than her using all my names was her calling me "young lady."

I smothered the sigh that tried to escape. I had learned the hard way that even a crabby sigh could get me grounded. "I'm sorry, Bubby. I'll take them over. I'm just going to take a quick shower and change first."

I needed to change into Vicky. But I didn't say that out loud.

Bubby picked up the eggplants and shoved them at me. "You will go *now*."

Before I could protest, she turned and left the kitchen. Conversation over.

I looked down at my shirt. I was covered in mud. I probably had dirt on my face and in my hair too.

Great.

Chapter Seven

I put the eggplants on the Patels' front porch. Then I rang the doorbell and turned to run. Just then the door opened. I hadn't even made it past the top step.

"Tori?" Jazzy asked. "Where are you going?"

I turned back and laughed. "Oh, I didn't want to get your house dirty,"

I said, looking down at my shirt. Jazzy just stared at me. She was probably wondering what I was even doing there.

"I brought eggplants for your grandmother," I explained. I bent down, picked them up and handed them to her.

"Eggplants? That's random," she said. I could tell she was confused.

"They're from my garden. I grew them."

"Really?" Her eyes were wide. Like she was really surprised.

I nodded. "I picked those ones today. And cucumbers for pickles. Tomatoes too."

"Wait," said Jazzy. She was holding the eggplants away from her. "Is there worm poop on these?"

"No," I said, laughing. "I rinsed them off. Anyway, it's not like regular poop."

She narrowed her eyes. "If it's what worms poop out, then it's poop."

That was true, I guess. "But it's not like dog poop. It's more like...fairy poop. Because it makes my garden grow better."

It was Jazzy's turn to laugh. She looked down at the eggplants in her hands again. "So you grew these. Right from seeds?"

"Yes," I said proudly. "I love botany—that's the study of plants. I'm going to be a food scientist when I grow up. There's nothing more important than food."

"That's really cool," Jazzy said. "What else do you grow?"

I started to list all the different plants in my garden. But then Mrs. Patel called to Jazzy from inside the house.

Jazzy rolled her eyes. "I'd better go."

"Me too," I said. I was beginning to think turning down dinner had been a big mistake.

I turned to leave.

"Hey, Tori?" Jazzy said.

I stopped and faced her again. "Yeah?" I was suddenly hoping she'd invite me for dinner. The *real* me. Tori.

"Tell Vicky I had a great time shopping today, okay?"

My throat got really tight, and I could feel the lump forming. All I could do was nod.

Then I ran home.

Chapter Eight

The next day I was in my garden, grumbling to myself about how fast weeds grow. They can pop up overnight, especially after a rain. I was so focused on my work, and grumbling, that I didn't notice anyone approaching. I was yanking out a dandelion when a shadow fell over my gloved hands.

Startled, I looked up. I had to squint to see Jazzy's face because the sun was shining behind her.

"Hi, Tori," she said. "Sorry, I didn't mean to scare you."

I tossed the weed into the wheelbarrow and sat back on my heels. I was happy for a break.

I was about to tell her that Vicky was busy. But I didn't feel like it. I was really starting to hate my fake sister.

"My grandparents are taking me to the Royal Botanical Gardens," Jazzy said.

Oh. The RBG is my very favorite place on earth. Especially the new rock garden. I know it sounds boring, but it's not only rocks. It has beautiful fountains and amazing plants and, of course, lots of cool boulders and rocks that are arranged in with the plants. I've only been there once, with my grandmother. Bubby left me there to explore as long as I wanted while she had tea in the café.

"Have fun!" I said.

She looked at me funny. "Wait... no, you don't get it. I came over here to invite you to come with us."

I got really excited for a second. Then she added, "Both of you. You *and* your sister."

Oh. Right. Of course Vicky was invited. *Vicky*, the girl Jazzy *really* wanted to hang out with. I almost said, *No thanks*. But then I thought about it. A trip to the RBG? I didn't want to pass that up.

Somehow I had to figure out how to make this work.

"Well, I'm sort of busy," I said, waving toward the garden. "But I bet Vicky will want to go with you. She'll probably need some time to get ready though."

Jazzy bit her lip and looked over her shoulder. Her grandparents were standing on the porch. They looked ready to go.

"Come on, girls!" Mrs. Patel called out. Yep, they were definitely ready to go.

Jazzy looked back at me. "I'll go get Vicky," she said.

"No!" I yelled, jumping up.

Jazzy jumped a little too. I smiled at her. "Sorry. I meant, *I'll* go get her." And then I called out to Mr. and Mrs. Patel. "We'll be right there!"

"Two minutes, Victoria!" Mrs. Patel answered.

I froze in my tracks. She'd just called me Victoria. Right in front of Jazzy! I was *so* busted.

"Dida!" Jazzy said. "It's Tori!"

Mrs. Patel shook her head. "Of course. I'm sorry, *Tori*. But we are *still* leaving in two minutes."

Jazzy turned back to me and rolled her eyes. "Even with her glasses on, she can't tell you from your sister."

I stared at Jazzy. I couldn't believe I hadn't just got caught.

"Well?" she said as she tapped her foot. "Hurry up!"

Once I was inside, I ran straight for the bathroom. One glance in the mirror told me there was no way I could turn myself into Vicky in two minutes. But I really didn't want to miss out on a trip to the gardens.

Jazzy had invited both of us, Tori *and* Vicky, so even though I knew I was not her first choice, maybe she wouldn't mind if only one of us went—me.

I didn't have time for a shower, but I hadn't been outside long enough to get *too* gross and sweaty. Grabbing the first clean clothes I could find, I quickly changed, used a bit of Bubby's deodorant and washed my hands and face.

"Vicky's not feeling great, so it's just me," I said to Jazzy. She was waiting on the porch. Her grandparents were already in their car.

"I thought you were too busy," Jazzy said, frowning at my outfit.

I looked down. I was wearing a pair of beige shorts and my favorite T-shirt, the black one that said, *I Grow My Own Food, What's Your Superpower?* Not the most fashionable clothes, but they were clean. Nothing with worm poop on it.

"I am. But I didn't want you to have to go by yourself with your grandparents," I said. I was trying hard not to care that she clearly hated my clothes.

But only half a second later, I couldn't pretend anymore. "Wait. What's wrong with what I'm wearing?"

She looked guilty, like I had caught her doing something bad. "Oh!" she said. "Nothing, it's just...I told your sister that pink and teal are her best colors, but that outfit is actually really cute on you."

I couldn't tell if she was being honest. Or making fun of me and my clothes. She didn't look like she was laughing. "Thanks?"

She grabbed my arm and led me across the yard. "Come on. Dadu will get upset if we don't hurry."

"Hey, Jazzy?" I said.

"Yeah?"

"Thanks for inviting me. I mean…" I swallowed because my mouth was suddenly very dry. "Thanks for inviting me *too*."

She stared at me for a second and then shrugged. "I figured you'd like going to the gardens. Even if it's just rocks."

I laughed. "It's not just rocks! Wait, you'll see."

Mrs. Patel's window rolled down. "Girls! Let's go!"

With a giggle, we ran toward the car and climbed into the back seat.

Chapter Nine

We arrived and got our passes at the front counter. Mr. and Mrs. Patel said we could explore on our own as long as we returned as soon as they texted us.

Jazzy and I smiled at each other. Her grandparents went into the café. I grabbed one of the garden maps from the counter and unfolded it.

"There's so much I want to show you!" I said as I looked at the map. "What do you want to see first?"

"I don't know," she said. "This seems like your kind of place. I'm just happy to be able to get away from my grandparents."

When I looked at her, she rolled her eyes. "Of course I love them, but they're starting to drive me a little crazy."

I laughed. "I know what you mean," I said. Bubby could get on my nerves sometimes. "My grandmother is nice, but she doesn't always get it."

"And you live with her *all* the time. I don't know how you do it. At least I will be leaving soon."

I hated being reminded. Even though once Jazzy moved to Australia, I could go back to being just one person. My life would be a lot less complicated. Which was a good thing.

But then I'd go back to being friendless. Right when school was starting. That was a bad thing.

As all this went through my head, Jazzy kept on talking. "Also, I'm going to be stuck with just them for the next three days. In *one* hotel room. With Dadu's snoring. So I'm glad you're here and they let us—"

I interrupted her. "Three days? In a hotel? Where are you going?" My voice sounded squeaky. I hadn't known she was going away.

She rolled her eyes again. "They're dragging me to Niagara Falls. Didn't I tell you?"

"Actually, Niagara Falls is pretty fun," I said, though I was thinking it would be more fun if we could *both* go.

Jazzy made a face. "What's so fun about water going over a cliff?"

It was funny she said that, because we were close to a waterfall. So close that I could see it through the big windows of the RBG building. But the garden feature was nothing like Niagara Falls. And anyway, going to Niagara was so much more than just seeing water going over a cliff.

I'd been there with my dad and Bubby the summer before, so I told Jazzy about all the cool things to do. You could visit the aviary to see all the birds. And there were museums, and you could go out on a boat that took you almost right up to the falls. Everyone got soaked from the mist, but it was really cool to get so close.

"That doesn't sound fun, getting soaked," Jazzy said, scrunching up her face.

"They give you a poncho."

She still didn't look impressed.

"It's fun!" I said. "Really."

"If you say so, Tori," she said, grabbing my hand as we went through the doors into the garden.

Right away, we were hit with earthy green smells. There were songbirds tweeting and singing. I could even hear the waterfall as it bubbled and gurgled.

I sighed in happiness. I was surrounded by my favorite things.

"Wow," Jazzy said. Her eyes were wide as she looked around the huge garden.

"Awesome, right?"

She looked at me. "It smells like worm poop."

My face fell. And then she laughed.

"Just kidding!" she said, tugging me down the path. "Show me where they grow the rocks."

"Grow the..."

Jazzy laughed again and squeezed my hand. “I’m joking, Tori. I know they don’t *grow* rocks.”

“Actually,” I said, “there are some plants that do *look* like rocks. They’re called lithops—maybe we’ll see some.”

She snorted. “Do you know *everything*?”

I felt my face heat up, but I sort of liked that she thought I was smart. “Not everything. Just a lot about plants.”

“And worms,” she said.

I smiled. “Come on. I’ll show you how cool a waterfall can be.”

It had been super hot at the RBG, so Mrs. Patel had said we could stop for ice cream. It was turning into a great day.

If it wasn’t for how bad I was feeling about lying to Jazzy, it probably would have been the best day ever.

She had really seemed to like being at the garden. With me. Not Vicky.

I wanted to tell her the truth. I had wanted to tell her about a hundred times that day. But every time I started to, I chickened out. First, because I knew she'd be mad and I wanted to spend the day at the RBG. And second, because it would have been weird if she got mad at me in front of her grandparents. And then because, well, ice cream.

"Tori, what kind are you getting?" Jazzy asked.

I was just sort of staring into the freezer filled with tubs.

I shrugged. "I can't decide. What are you having?"

She made a face. "I don't know. I kind of want strawberry. But the chocolate cheesecake looks good too."

"Hey," I said. "Why don't you get one in a dish and I'll get the other? Then we can share."

Suddenly Jazzy's arm was around my shoulders. "See?" she said as I looked at her. I was trying not to cross my eyes, but she was really close. "This is why we're best friends."

That made my heart flutter in happiness. But then I remembered.

"I thought you were best friends with Vicky." I said it softly so her grandparents wouldn't hear.

Jazzy pulled me close and whispered into my ear. "Would she have shared ice cream with me?"

"No," I said, shaking my head. "She's selfish like that. Also, she doesn't like strawberries."

Jazzy gave me a smile. "That's what I thought. Good thing you're here."

None of this made any sense. How could Jazzy possibly know my fake sister was selfish?

I suddenly felt guilty. Because not only had I made up a sister, but now

I was trash-talking her. To the girl I'd lied to.

I might have been Jazzy's current best friend, but she didn't know the truth. And the truth was that I was a horrible best friend.

I was a pretty lousy fake sister too.

Chapter Ten

Two days later, with Jazzy gone to Niagara Falls, I was bored. Very bored.

And lonely.

So lonely that I was sitting in my shed, talking to my worms. Talking to plants helps them, because humans breathe out what plants breathe in, but talking to worms doesn't help the worms. As far as I know.

Also, they never talk back. Or get your jokes.

But Dad was at work and Bubby was inside playing mah-jongg with her old lady friends in the rec room. That meant I couldn't even watch TV.

So I was hanging out with my worms. I'd already done the day's weeding and harvesting, so there was nothing left to do in the garden. I'd even cleaned all my tools and taken a pile of cherry tomatoes in to my grandmother and her friends.

They'd oohed and ahhed but then quickly returned to their game. The tiles made clacking noises as they moved them around. When the ladies got noisy and started laughing about old-lady stuff, I went back to my shed.

I took my phone out of my pocket. No new messages from Jazzy. The night before she'd texted me to tell me I'd been right. Niagara Falls *was* fun. She'd even sent me some pictures. My favorite was the one from the aviary. Jazzy had a bright red and green parrot on her shoulder. Across the photo she'd written *Me and my second-best friend!*

I tried not to feel jealous. But it was hard knowing she was having such a good time. And I was stuck talking to worms.

I had an idea. I stuck my hand deep into the worm bin and pulled one out. "Hi there, Wiggles," I said, wiping some of the dirt off it.

I placed the worm on my shoulder and took a selfie. The worm wiggled off and fell onto the floor. I scooped it up and put it back into the bin. "See ya, Wiggles."

Then I sent the selfie to Jazzy.

> ***Check out me and MY second-best friend!***

Only a few minutes later, I got a reply.

So funny!

Then she filled my screen with hearts and smilies and thumbs-up emojis.

I sent her a wink and asked how it was going.

Amazing! Having fun, even with the old people! Tell Vicky I say hi!

Oh right, my fake sister. Jazzy couldn't text her directly because I'd told her Vicky didn't have a phone.

I will.

Coming back tomorrow.

I sent her a thumbs-up.

And then we will have the most EPIC sleepover.

Wait, what?

What sleepover?

At your place! Sorry, gotta go. Ask your bubby.

And with that she was gone.

But what had she been talking about? Who was behind this sleep-over idea?

There was no way we—me and my fake sister—could have a sleepover with Jazzy!

Once I saw the last of the old ladies drive away, I went back into the house.

Bubby was in the kitchen, standing at the sink. She was washing a big platter, the one she always serves bagels on.

"Hi, Bubby," I said, coming up beside her and stealing a strawberry off the fruit tray.

She smiled. "There you are. Can you help me clean up, *bubeleh*? That fruit goes in the fridge, and the table needs clearing."

I nodded but didn't move. "Jazzy said something about a sleepover?"

"Oh yes. I'm sorry—I forgot to tell you. Her grandparents have tickets for the theater tomorrow night, so she's staying here. I knew you girls would like that, so I told the Patels we'd love to have her."

Uh-uh, no way.

"No, thanks," I said.

"Pardon?" Bubby blinked and then frowned. "No, thanks *what*?"

"I don't want Jazzy to stay here."

Bubby put the platter into the dish rack and dried her hands. "Why not? I thought you two were friends."

"We are," I said. "But not *sleepover* friends."

"What does that mean?"

I had no idea. I was making it up as I went along. "It means…uh…that Jazzy has some weird habits."

Bubby tilted her head. "What kind of weird habits?"

Yes, Tori, what kind of weird habits?

"I mean, *I* have weird habits. And I'm worried she'll hear me snore. Or that I might wet the bed."

Obviously, I was getting desperate.

My grandmother lifted an eyebrow. Just one—which was enough to make me fidget. "As the person who does your laundry, I know you haven't wet the bed since you were four." She crossed her arms. "And you don't snore unless you're sick."

I sniffled, but that just made both of her eyebrows go up.

"What's going on here, young lady?"

Uh-oh, she'd skipped past my full name and right to *young lady*.

"I...I just don't want her to sleep over, that's all."

"But you used to have Anna sleep over all the time."

"That was Anna," I said with a shrug.

Bubby sighed. "I don't understand, Tori. But either way, I've already told her grandparents that we'd watch her while they're away. You're just going to have to make the best of it, I'm sorry."

Jazzy was going to be sleeping at my house! How could I possibly hide that I didn't really have a twin sister? I didn't have a clone. I didn't have a robot. I didn't even have a life-sized doll.

And how would I keep Bubby and my dad from finding out this whole story I'd made up?

I was going to have to figure out how to make my fake twin sister real.

Or I was going to have to tell the truth.

Either way, I was doomed.

Chapter Eleven

The next day I asked my grandmother to take me to the garden center.

Then the hardware store.

And finally the grocery store. Because epic sleepovers need snacks, right?

But the *real* reason I had Bubby running all over town was that I didn't want to be home when Jazzy returned from Niagara Falls.

Because I was dreading the sleepover.

Actually, I was still hoping that I would somehow come up with a way to get out of the sleepover.

But by the time we got home from shopping, I hadn't thought of anything.

And Jazzy wasn't home from Niagara Falls yet. But she would be soon.

And that epic sleepover? It was happening. Whether I wanted it to or not.

So there I was, kneeling on the couch, looking out the front window. I was waiting for the Patels' big car to pull into their driveway.

I'd been there since Jazzy had texted to say they were on their way. With every minute, I got more nervous.

My grandmother was in the den with her iPad, watching cat videos or something. Every once in a while I'd hear her laugh. If I wasn't so worried about the sleepover, I would have been in there too. I like funny cat videos too. Sometimes we watch them together.

But I was way too nervous. And anyway, I needed to figure out how I was going to handle this. Dad was out on the front lawn, crisscrossing the grass with the mower.

How on earth was I going to keep Jazzy from mentioning Vicky to my dad or grandmother?

How was I going to get through this night without getting busted, grounded and probably, worst of all, losing the one friend I had?

There was no way. Unless I could arrange things so they didn't talk to each other at all.

Although that still didn't solve my problem of a made-up sister.

But one problem at a time.

The loud hum of the lawn mower stopped. My dad was standing on the sidewalk, talking to Ms. Simon from across the street. Maisey and Daisy were coloring on the sidewalk with chalk. I looked at the twins.

Real twins, not like me and Vicky.

It seemed like Dad was telling her a story. His hands were waving around wildly as he talked.

Ms. Simon laughed and reached out to touch Dad's arm. That seemed like a friendly thing to do.

Very friendly. I noticed that Dad had a big smile on his face.

That gave me an idea.

But I had to act fast. I jumped off the couch and ran to the front hall. I slid my feet into my flip-flops and hurried out the door. Then I walked as quickly as I could (without running) down the front porch steps and right up to Dad and Ms. Simon.

"Hi!" I said.

"Hi, Tori," Ms. Simon said.

"What's up?" Dad asked.

"Dad, I was just thinking," I said. "You know how you said you wanted to see that new movie?"

Dad blinked a few times. "I did?"

"Yes," I said and then looked at Ms. Simon and rolled my eyes. Dad had no idea what I was talking about. But *she* didn't know that! "You know, that new one. C'mon, Dad…you remember, with the…" I waved at him.

But he wasn't catching on.

"The superhero one?" Ms. Simon said. "It looks really good."

"Yes!" I said. "That one. Exactly."

Dad blinked some more.

"I was hoping to see that one," said Ms. Simon. "I have a thing for action movies."

Yes! I could have hugged her. Did she know what I was trying to do? I had no idea, but so far it was working.

"You should totally go," I said. "Both of you."

Dad's eyes went wide. "Uhh..."

"Together," I said very slowly so he would catch on. "*Tonight*."

I looked at Ms. Simon. She was looking at my dad, waiting for his answer. *She* seemed to think it was a good idea.

But my dad looked like a fish that had flopped out of the water, gasping for air. I nudged him with my elbow.

"Oh, sorry," he said. His face was red. I didn't think it was from the sun. "Uh, sure. Want to go with us, Miriam?"

With *us*? No!

"Dad," I said calmly, trying not to panic. "Jazzy's coming for a sleepover. I can't go."

He looked at me. His face was a jumble of emotions. "Oh, well..."

"We could go," Ms. Simon suggested. "Just you and me, Zack. You know, like a date." When Dad didn't answer she laughed, but it didn't sound real. "Just kidding! *Not* a date. That was a joke. Ha ha!"

Then Dad laughed, but it sounded fake too. His eyes didn't wrinkle at the corners like they usually do.

Holy awkward grown-ups.

"You two work it out," I said and then hurried back into the house.

I wanted to pump my fists up in the air, but that would raise suspicions. I didn't want them to know this was all part of my plan.

The plan that was going perfectly.

For now.

Chapter Twelve

I returned to my spot on the couch so I could watch through the window as my dad and Ms. Simon kept talking.

I couldn't tell what they were saying, but Dad wasn't using his hands anymore. In fact, he'd stuffed them into the pockets of his jeans.

Ms. Simon was smiling and nodding. Maybe they were making plans. Maybe they'd go out for dinner and everything. Like a real date.

Though I couldn't tell if either of them wanted it to be one. Maybe. Maybe they'd fall in love.

Whatever. Not my focus right now. I just needed Dad out of the house. With that plan in action, now I had to figure out how to get rid of my grandmother.

But before I could come up with anything, Dad and Ms. Simon nodded at each other and went their separate ways. She crossed the street to her house. Dad, instead of returning to his mowing, walked toward our front door.

Not wanting to get busted for spying on them, I hurried into the den.

Sure enough, Bubby was watching a video of a cat riding a vacuum. The cat was wearing a shark suit. We'd seen it before, but it still made both of us laugh.

"We need a cat in a shark suit," I said.

Bubby smiled at me. "If only your father didn't have allergies."

I pointed at the screen. "Well, we'd also have the Roomba to clean up the hair."

She snorted. Just then Dad appeared in the doorway.

"We need to talk," he said.

Four words that I hate when they are put together. Especially when Dad's arms are crossed and he is frowning, like now. Because it almost always means I am about to get in trouble.

"Should I leave?" Bubby asked.

Dad shook his head as he leaned against the door frame. "No, this is the same thing we talked about the other day."

My heart began to pound really hard. I was *so* getting busted. They knew about Vicky and all the lies.

I braced myself for a lecture. And a grounding.

"Tori," Dad began. Then he looked down, like he was trying to choose the right words. He sighed and then, after a long pause, said, "We know you've been missing your mom."

"Huh?" I asked. *Again?*

"Or maybe..." He looked up at the ceiling. "Maybe you're missing having *a* mom."

I thought my grandmother would be as confused as I was, but when I looked over at her, she was nodding. She seemed to know what was going on. She looked sad, not confused.

"No," I said. "That's not...um...no."

"I told him," Bubby said. "About the shirt."

Now Dad was nodding. He turned to Bubby and said, "Tori just tried to set me up with Miriam Simon."

Bubby snorted and then tried to cover it up with a cough. "Oh, well," she said. "That's...interesting."

"Mom," Dad said to her. "I don't need to be set up. Especially by my daughter."

The fact that he hadn't had a date in forever said maybe he *did* need to be set up. And if not by me, then who?

"Anyway," Dad said, sounding kind of sad, "this isn't about me."

"I thought you would like to go out with her," I said. "You just needed a little help to make it happen."

Dad pushed away from the doorway and sat down on the oversized chair where I love to curl up and read my gardening books. He patted the spot beside him—yes, the chair is that big. When I sat down he put his arm around me and pulled me in for a side hug.

"I hope you don't feel like you're missing out because you don't have a mom."

"I don't," I said. It was the truth. I couldn't miss what I'd never had. I'd only ever known my mother from pictures or what other people had told me about her. I didn't even really get sad when I thought about her. "I just figured you and Ms. Simon might have a nice time. You like her, don't you?"

"I don't really know her. She seems nice, I suppose." He looked at me. "But you're sure this isn't about your mom?"

"I'm very sure." I said firmly. "Anyway, I have Bubby, who is like a mom."

"Well, as moms go, I guess she's an *okay* mom," he teased. I knew for a fact that he thought she was the best mom ever.

Bubby gave Dad a very stern look. "What did you say, young man?" Even though I knew she'd heard him perfectly well.

"Uh-oh, Dad," I said. "She's giving you the *young man*. Watch out you don't get grounded! You have a date."

"It's not a date," Dad said. And then he scrunched up his eyebrows. "Is it?"

Bubby shrugged, then winked at me.

"It's *totally* a date," I said. "Also, you should probably take her out after the movie. Like to a café or something. Ladies like that."

He frowned. "What do you know about all that?"

"Please," I said. "Bubby and I watch *The Bachelor*."

"About that," he said.

"She's right," Bubby interrupted. "You should take her for coffee after. Maybe something sweet. Too bad you don't have time for a haircut."

Dad stood up. "I've heard just about enough from you two for one day. I'd better go finish mowing the lawn."

Bubby and I laughed as we heard him grumbling all the way down the hall.

My plan was turning out much better than I had hoped. I'd only meant to get him out of the house, but maybe I'd done something good at the same time.

One down, one to go.

But how was I going to get Bubby out of the house?

"So," I said with a big smile. "Maybe *you* should get a date too. For tonight!"

She snorted again. "I went along with your little plan with your father because he does need to get out more. And I like Miriam. But it's not going to work on me."

"What do you mean?" I said, making my eyes wide. "I don't have a plan."

She looked at me. Clearly she wasn't buying it.

"Well, *I'm* not going anywhere, Tori," she said. "Just what are you and Jasvitha up to?"

Well, Jazzy wasn't up to anything, but I couldn't exactly say that.

Just then a car honked next door. Saved by the bell. Jazzy and her grandparents were home.

Chapter Thirteen

I jumped up and started running for the bathroom, hoping to avoid seeing Jazzy.

But then I realized she might ring the doorbell and ask my grandmother for Tori *and* Vicky. Ugh.

So I ran out the back door and around the house. Jazzy was just walking up my front steps.

"Hey!" I said before she could get to the door. "How was the trip?"

She had a big smile on her face. "Hey, Tori! It was amazing! You were right about Niagara Falls being super fun. Or wait..." She paused. "Maybe it was *Vicky* who told me it was a fun place?"

"It was me," I said, happy to be able to tell her at least one honest thing.

"Ready for tonight?" she asked. "I came over to ask if I can bring anything."

I shook my head. "We picked up some snacks already, and Bubby said we can order pizza."

"Awesome!" she said. "I got some snacks too. And gifts."

"Gifts?"

"Souvenirs." She rolled her eyes. "From Niagara Falls."

How cool! I never expected that she would bring me something back from her trip. I was about to ask her what it was, but she spoke first.

"Something for each of you."

Oh. Right. Of course she would get something for me and my "sister." My stomach did a flip.

"Where is Vicky anyway?" Jazzy asked, looking around.

Yes, Tori. Where is *Vicky?* I wanted to blurt out the truth right then. Jazzy would get mad, but at least I could stop lying.

But then I thought about how we were stuck together for this sleepover. Now was not the best time to make her hate me.

I watched Dad, who was still pushing the mower around. I thought about his date with Ms. Simon. For some reason I suddenly wondered who would be looking after her kids.

"Babysitting," I blurted out, rather proud of myself for my quick thinking.

"Oh yeah?" Jazzy said. "For who?"

"Ms. Simon," I said, nodding toward her house. As soon as I said it, I wished

I'd said Vicky was babysitting across town or something. Because what if Jazzy spoke to Ms. Simon?

More people I couldn't let talk to each other. It was all so exhausting! I was going to miss Jazzy, but I was also relieved that she'd be leaving in a week.

"Where is Ms. Simon going?" Jazzy asked.

"Actually, she's going out with my dad. They're going to a movie."

Jazzy's eyes lit up. "Oh! Like a date?"

I nodded. "Yeah. He hasn't been on a date in forever."

"That's cute. But it's too bad Vicky can't hang out with us."

"Yeah," I said. *Too bad.*

"We were going to have so much fun," said Jazzy.

"We can still have fun. You and me," I said, a little hurt.

Jazzy quickly hugged me. "Of course we will! The best, most epic fun!"

"Hello, Tori." Mrs. Patel poked her head out of their front door and waved. "Jasvitha, come unpack your bag. Dadu and I have to leave soon, and then you will have all evening to play."

"Yes, Dida," Jazzy said as she gave me a tiny eye roll. "I'd better go. But see you soon! It's going to be awesome!"

I still wasn't sure how I was going to keep her away from my grandmother, but I guessed we'd just have to see.

Chapter Fourteen

I had never seen my dad so nervous. Then again, I had never seen him getting ready for a date before.

He shaved and then asked Bubby and me to help him choose which cologne to put on. We both liked the one we'd bought him for Father's Day the best. Then he asked us to help him figure out what to wear.

It was cute seeing him like that. And, I have to admit, I was a little nervous for him.

Helping him get ready took my mind off Jazzy coming over. When the doorbell rang, I jumped. But then I remembered and got nervous for a whole different reason.

"I'll get it," I said, hoping I could take Jazzy directly to my room. I didn't want to give her the chance to talk to anyone.

But when I answered the door, it wasn't her. It was Ms. Simon.

"Oh hi, Tori," she said. She looked as nervous and fidgety as Dad was.

"Come on in," I said. "All ready for your date?"

She suddenly looked like she'd eaten something gross. She leaned toward me and whispered, "Does your dad think this is a date?"

I nodded. "But no pressure. I don't need a new mom."

Her eyes went wide in alarm. I felt bad for teasing her.

"I'm just kidding," I said.

Ms. Simon swallowed hard and said, "Right, ha ha." She looked down the hall. "Um, so…is your dad here? I was ready, so I thought I'd pop over."

"I'll get him." But then I had a thought. "So who's watching your kids tonight?"

She tilted her head. "They're with their dad for the weekend. Why?"

I couldn't exactly tell her why I was curious. "Oh, I don't know." I shrugged. "I was just thinking that maybe I could babysit sometime." Actually, I wouldn't mind. Daisy and Maisey are pretty cute.

She smiled. "Thank you, Tori, I will keep that in mind. I'm sure the girls would love that."

"Miriam, hi," my dad said as he stepped into the hall.

"Hi, Zack," said Ms. Simon. "I was early, so I came over. I hope you don't mind. Tori's been keeping me company."

Dad came up and gave me a side hug. "Thanks, Tori." He grabbed his keys from the hook by the door. "We should get going. Tori, don't give your grandmother too much trouble tonight, okay?"

"Does that mean you'll be staying out really late?" I asked.

Ms. Simon and Dad looked at each other. They both looked uncomfortable.

"Because you can," I said quickly. "I don't mind. And I already told Ms. Simon that I don't need a new mom, so tonight is all about you two having fun."

Dad gave me a stern look that I knew meant *just stop talking*. So I did. Other than to wish them a great date night, of course.

Chapter Fifteen

Bubby was back in the den, looking at stuff on her iPad, and I was downstairs setting up the rec room when the doorbell rang again.

This time it had to be Jazzy. I was glad, because I was getting hungry. Since I didn't know what she liked on her pizza, it had seemed rude to order before she arrived.

I ran up the stairs. "I'll get it!" I yelled.

"Whoa," I said as I opened the door. Jazzy looked like she was packed and ready to leave home for good. Her backpack, slung over one shoulder, was stuffed and had a pillow poking out of the top. A purple shopping bag was hanging off her wrist, and she was holding a giant bakery box in both hands. "Can I help?"

"Can you take this?" She pushed the box at me and kicked the door closed behind her. "We stopped at the sweet shop on the way home—samosas and ladoos."

"Oh yum," I said. I love Indian treats.

"Dida said that samosas are your favorite."

I nodded, my mouth already watering just thinking about the fried pastries. I turned to take the box to the kitchen.

"And I know that coconut ladoos are Vicky's favorite."

I froze in place. "What?"

"Your sister. Ladoos are her favorite Indian treat."

How could that be? I suppose if I had a twin sister she might love ladoos, but I *didn't* have a twin sister. So how could Jazzy know what her favorite treat was? I'd sure never told her that. Especially since I hate coconut.

I looked over my shoulder at her, but Jazzy was just smiling at me. She kicked off her flip-flops and put her backpack down.

"I..." I cleared my throat. I was going to ask her how she knew about Vicky's favorite treat, but I was suddenly afraid of her answer. I chickened out. "I'm going to take these into the kitchen. Want something to drink?"

"Sure," she said, following me. "And then we should go take Vicky some snacks. I bet she's hungry by now."

"What?" I said again, sliding the box onto the kitchen counter.

Jazzy was nodding. "I know when I babysit I get *so* hungry. Especially if they don't have good snacks. We should go visit her."

"No," I said. "I don't think Ms. Simon would like it if she had a bunch of people over. She's supposed to be watching the kids."

"She still has to eat," Jazzy insisted. "I'm sure it will be fine if we don't stay long."

"I don't know," I said. "Maybe later, after we get the pizza."

She looked at me for a long moment. I had a weird feeling that she was trying to get me to say something.

"Hey, tell me about your trip." That probably wasn't it.

She started telling me all about Niagara Falls and everything she'd done there.

"Oh yeah!" she said suddenly. "Presents!" She ran to the front hall and came back with the purple bag.

I have to admit, I was pretty excited. At least, for *my* gift. Who knew how Vicky was going to feel about hers?

"It's nothing big. I got you a T-shirt," she said, holding it up in front of her. "It's not Niagara Fallsy, but it was so you that I couldn't resist."

It was sunshine yellow and had a picture of a smiling worm on it. Beside the worm it said *Casting Call*.

I squealed in excitement. "OMG! I love it!" I reached out to grab it. I really did love it. A lot. Like, so much I could barely stand not putting it on immediately.

"I didn't get the joke at first," Jazzy said. "I saw the worm, so I knew you'd like it. Then Dadu reminded me that castings are worm poop, so I knew you wouldn't just like it. You would *love* it!"

I smiled at her. "I *do* love it!" I gave her a hug. "Thank you so much, Jazzy!"

"You're welcome. But wait," she said. "Do you think Vicky will like *her* present?"

"I'm sure she will," I said. I was about to go show Bubby my new T-shirt.

"You don't even know what it is though."

"No…but…" I fumbled. "You have such good taste, I'm sure she'll like whatever you got."

Jazzy lifted her eyebrows.

"I mean, yes, of course I'd love to see it!" I added.

She smiled and pulled another T-shirt out of the bag.

It was teal and pink and had a picture of the falls on it. The water was sparkly with glitter. It was pretty nice. If you're into teal and pink and glitter.

Which I guess Vicky is.

"She'll love that," I said.

"I know, right?"

My stomach decided that now was a good time to change the subject. It growled. Loudly.

Jazzy laughed. "That means pizza time, right?"

I nodded. "We should put in our order. What do you like on yours?"

"Pineapple and mushroom. Oh, and green peppers. What do you like?"

"That sounds good to me. I'll eat almost anything on pizza." I made a face. "Except olives. I hate olives."

"Me too. But what about Vicky? Doesn't she *love* olives?"

"Um, no."

She tilted her head. "Are you sure? I'm pretty sure she told me she loves olives."

Huh? When would she have said that? Wait, why was I even thinking like this? I was starting to think Jazzy had been hit on the head or something.

"I don't think so…"

"We should probably get olives on half," Jazzy said. "For her."

"She's not even eating with us," I said, starting to panic. Because how was I going to explain olives to my grandmother when *nobody* in my family (nobody who is a real person, that is) likes them?

"But we are going to take some over to her, aren't we?"

Not if I can help it.

"Maybe," I said. "But when they put olives on, the juice gets everywhere, and I don't want to taste even a little. Even if they are her favorite…" I was starting to sound crazy. "Vicky can go without. You know, this one time."

Jazzy stared at me for a moment. Then she nodded and said okay. Even though Vicky would be sad, she added.

I pulled open the kitchen junk drawer to get the pizza menu. I was really starting to hate Vicky.

The pizza arrived, and we dove in. We were nearly done when Jazzy announced we should take Vicky some coconut ladoos.

I didn't even want to think about more food, since I'd eaten way too much pizza. I'd thought if we finished the whole thing (Bubby hadn't wanted any), there wouldn't be any to take to Vicky. *Taa daa.* No reason to go over to Ms. Simon's house. I'd stuffed so much in my face I was starting to feel ill.

I'd been keeping Jazzy so busy in my basement with eating and watching shows that I thought she'd forgotten about my fake sister.

Nope. And I'd forgotten about the treats Jazzy had brought over.

"She's fine," I said, dropping the last crust on my plate. I could not eat even one more nibble. "I'm sure she'll enjoy the ladoos even more tomorrow."

Jazzy shook her head. "No, we should go now."

"I can't," I said, panicking again. And it wasn't just about the giant ball of pizza in my gut. Although I was starting to worry about that too. "I…" I faltered, trying to come up with an excuse. "I have to take a bath. Yep, it's my bath day. Vicky will understand."

Bath day? Ugh, Tori, you are so dumb.

Jazzy stared at me for a long time. "Well, I'm going to go over with the snacks," she announced.

"You probably shouldn't," I said. "Ms. Simon won't like it."

She huffed out a big sigh and rolled her eyes. "Whatever. You go take your bath. I will take the ladoos over when I'm done here."

I looked at her plate. She still had almost a whole slice of pizza left. While I'd been stuffing my face, she'd been eating slowly. Like a normal person.

"Fine. Go," I said, jumping up off the couch. "By yourself. I'll be in the bathroom. In a bath. By myself."

"You're weird sometimes, Tori," Jazzy said.

I held my breath. I couldn't tell if she meant good weird or bad weird.

"Well?" she said. "Are you going to go take that bath that's so important or what?"

Chapter Sixteen

I ran up the stairs and into the bathroom. I was so panicked that I turned on the taps before I even realized it.

"What are you doing?" Bubby asked from the doorway.

Isn't it obvious? "Taking a bath," I said.

"Now? With your friend downstairs?"

"I got some pizza sauce on me,"

I said. Even just the word *pizza* was enough to make me feel gross. More gross. "Jazzy is still eating, and then she has to run home for a minute. But she's coming right back. So don't worry when you hear her leave."

She squinted at me for a second. I checked the water temperature and put the plug into the bottom of the tub. Now that I was calming down a bit, a new plan was forming. This could still work out!

"All right," Bubby said finally. "I'll leave you girls alone."

Whew.

I closed and locked the door. Then I unlocked the bathroom window and opened it. I gently pushed the screen out. It clattered a bit as it fell to the ground, hitting the big garbage can on the way. I froze, waiting for the sound of Bubby's footsteps.

Nothing.

I caught a glimpse of my new T-shirt in the mirror. Yikes! I had changed into it while we were waiting for the pizza to arrive. But I couldn't wear that and pretend to be Vicky!

I checked the hamper. It was empty except for the gross T-shirt Dad had worn to mow the lawn.

Great. That meant I had two choices, Bubby's ratty old bathrobe or Dad's smelly old thing.

It wasn't much of a choice. I pulled my new T-shirt off, stuffed it between some folded towels in the linen closet and tugged Dad's shirt on over my head.

It smelled like him and grass and… ugh…who knew what, but at least the bath would be ready for me when I got back.

I turned the water off and double-checked that the door was locked. Taking a deep breath and praying that I didn't get caught or hurt, I climbed up on the bathroom counter. I took one more breath and then I went out the window.

I landed lightly on the garbage can and then hopped down to the ground. I jogged across the street to the side of Ms. Simon's house. I hid behind the bushes in a spot where I could see my front door.

I waited.

I didn't have to wait long. Soon the front door opened and out came Jazzy, the bakery box in her hands.

My stomach gurgled uncomfortably. I wondered if I'd ever be able to eat pizza again. I seriously doubted it.

As Jazzy approached the front porch, I stepped out of the bushes. I hoped it looked like I was just coming around from the backyard.

"Oh, hi!" I said with a smile and a wave. "What are you doing here?"

"Hey, Vicky!" she said, smiling back. Then she noticed my shirt. She frowned. "That's an interesting fashion choice."

I looked down. "I didn't want to wear any of my fashionable clothes babysitting. These kids are messy. You know how it is."

She nodded. "Oh yeah, for sure. Anyway, I came to bring you a treat and say hi. I'm sorry you can't hang out with me and Tori tonight."

"That's okay," I said. "I don't mind babysitting. Daisy and Maisey are good kids. Other than being messy, I mean."

Jazzy looked behind me. "So where are they?"

"Oh. They're already in bed, fast asleep," I said. I lowered my voice. "So we should probably be quiet. I was just hanging out in the backyard because it's such a nice night."

Jazzy nodded. "Well, I was going to bring you some pizza too, but your sister ate it all."

"Oh, well," I said, laughing, "she does love her food, you know." *Just not usually quite so much of it.*

"Anyway," said Jazzy. "I brought you some coconut ladoos, because I know they're your favorite."

She opened the box. Yup, there were six little pastries in there. "Great, thanks!" I said. "I'll enjoy these later."

"No, you should totally eat them now."

You will barf if you take even one tiny bite, my stomach warned.

"No, I'm okay," I said. "But I should get back inside. Check on the kids."

"C'mon, Vicky," Jazzy said. "I got them just for you. You have to try at least one. Coconut is your very favorite, and these are so fresh and delicious."

As I looked into my friend's eyes, I realized there was no getting out of this. I could either tell her the truth or I could eat a coconut ladoo.

It was not an easy choice.

With a deep breath and an apology to my stomach, I plucked one of the little balls out of the box and popped it into my mouth.

I forced a smile onto my face as I chewed and chewed. It was really coconutty and *so* sweet. It turned to sugary goo in my mouth. "Mmm! Delicious!" I said through the mouthful of food, not caring how rude it was. "Thank you! Maybe you could take the rest home for me. I'll eat them tomorrow."

She pushed the box toward me. "You sure you don't want any more?"

I turned my head, trying not to gag at the coconut smell. "Nope, I'm good. Thanks though. Gotta go—I think I hear one of the kids crying!"

I ran around the back of the house and barfed as quietly as I could into Ms. Simon's lilac bushes.

Chapter Seventeen

I gave myself a couple of minutes for some deep breaths and to make sure I was done puking. Then I ran back to my house. I used the recycle bin as a step up to the garbage can and climbed back through the bathroom window. No time to brush my teeth, so I just swished some toothpaste and water around in my mouth. I took off my clothes and threw them into the hamper.

Then I jumped into the bath. Yikes! The water was not even close to warm. I added some more hot water.

After a quick wash, I got out and dried off. I towel-dried my hair and put on Bubby's bathrobe. I opened the door quietly and crept down the hall to my bedroom. I quickly put on my pajamas.

I was so tired. I just wanted to crawl into bed and go to sleep, but it was barely eight o'clock. Instead I went downstairs to join Jazzy. She was on the couch, scrolling through Netflix.

I dropped down beside her.

"How was your bath?" she asked.

"Great. Very relaxing."

"Aren't you going to ask how your sister is?"

"Sure, I guess," I said. Jazzy sounded weird. I figured she was still mad.

"She's good. The kids are making her crazy though."

"Huh?"

Jazzy turned her head to look at me. "They've been fighting nonstop since she got there. She was so glad to see me but wished I'd brought her some pizza."

Um, what?

"Anyway," Jazzy continued, turning back to the TV, "she loved the ladoos. She ate them all."

Why was Jazzy lying? I was about to ask but then realized that if I did, *I'd* be busted. Because how could I *know* she was lying? I suddenly wasn't so sure I wanted to be friends with someone who lied so much.

Almost as much as *I'd* been lying. Ugh. I was so confused.

"Sounds about right," I said. "Vicky does love her coconut ladoos!"

We stared at the screen for a while. Then Jazzy turned the TV off and turned toward me. Not just her head, but her whole body. She sat facing me now, cross-legged. "So, Tori, I have some amazing news!"

"Oh yeah?" I said.

She nodded. "My parents called earlier. They're having trouble finding a place in Australia, so they're renting a condo for now. But it's only one bedroom, so..."

My brain was having trouble figuring out what she was getting at. And how this was awesome news. "So...?"

She rolled her eyes. "So they thought it would be best if I stayed here for the school year!"

"Here? Like in my basement?"

Jazzy frowned. Then her eyes went wide. "Tori! No. I mean living with my grandparents next door. But that means we'll get to go to school together. I'm *not* leaving next week! Isn't that awesome?"

Not exactly.

"Oh," I said. "That's...wow...that's great." Except that it wasn't. Or maybe it would have been if it wasn't for my big, fat, giant, stupid lie.

"You don't seem very happy," she said. "I thought you'd be excited. Vicky was super pumped when I told her!"

Another lie! But, of course, one I couldn't bust her on. This was all getting so complicated!

I stared at her, trying to figure it all out. I *couldn't* be two people. I'd barely managed it for a week!

I had to tell her the truth. Even if it meant she would hate me. Yeah, she was definitely going to hate me.

"I..." I sighed and then started again. "Jazzy, I have to tell you something."

"It had better be that you're a lot more excited than you seem to be," she said.

"I am, but...I have to be honest..." *Oh jeez. How do I do this?* "You see, well...Vicky is...well, it's like...she's not a real person."

"What?" Jazzy asked, eyes wide again.

I looked down at my hands. "You and I first met when I was all dressed up. Then when you met me that second time in the garden, you didn't recognize me! I thought *you* thought I was gross and dirty." I started to cry. I couldn't help it. "I was scared you wouldn't like me. A girl who digs in the garden and hates teal and pink. But that's the real me. My fancy, fashion-forward sister Vicky doesn't exist."

"So wait. You're saying you *made up* a twin sister?"

I nodded. "Yeah. I'm really sorry. I just wanted you to like me. But then everything got so confusing."

"You thought I would only like *Vicky*."

"I guess so. Yeah."

"Even though she doesn't exist."

I shrugged.

"That doesn't make any sense!"

I looked up at her. "Not now it doesn't. But at the time?" I sighed again. "No, it didn't make sense then either. I was just a chicken and thought you liked the fake me better. I don't know why. But my best friend just moved away, and I was lonely. I...I just wanted a friend."

Jazzy sighed.

I used the sleeve of my pj's to wipe away my tears. "I understand if you hate me."

"I don't hate you," she said. "In fact, what would you say if I told you I knew all along?"

My head snapped up. She was grinning at me. Like it was funny. Which it totally wasn't.

"*What?*" I said. "Since when?"

She shrugged. "Pretty much from the beginning."

Suddenly I was *so* mad. I couldn't decide if I wanted to yell at her or run away. "Are you serious? You've been tricking me this—" I stopped talking as it sunk in. "Wow. I've been tricking *you* this whole time. I'm sorry, Jazzy. I'm a total jerk."

All of a sudden Jazzy's arms were around me. "You're not a total jerk. I was mean to you when I met you in your garden. I didn't understand what you were doing, but when you explained it all and showed me all the cool stuff at the RBG, I got it. I think you're smart and cool, and I like you. *You*, Tori, not some fake girl you *think* I would like."

"Really?"

She nodded. "And to be honest, I thought you would have fessed up way before now." She laughed.

"I almost did," I admitted. "A few times. But I was so scared you'd hate me. I thought maybe I could keep it up until you left, and then it wouldn't matter."

She snorted. "I wouldn't have let you. Didn't you wonder about all the crazy things I was saying and doing? The shirts, the olives, the coconut ladoos?"

"Which I barfed up, by the way."

"WHAT?"

I nodded. "I ate so much pizza and then, ugh, I *really* hate coconut."

She laughed again. "Why do you think I bought them?"

"You're evil," I said. I was smiling now.

"Not really. I just wanted you to come clean. I didn't really understand why you did it, but now I do. I'm sorry I made you feel like you had to pretend to be someone else to be my friend."

"And I'm sorry you bought that T-shirt I'll never wear."

"Pffft," she said, waving me off. "I bought that for me. So yeah, I'll take it back, thank you. Although it would have been funny to see you wearing it, knowing you hate it."

I rolled my eyes. "Maybe a little."

"So…Tori? We're good, right?"

"More than good," I said, my voice a bit squeaky. I was so relieved and happy, and this was all going better than I could have imagined. Except for barfing in the bushes, of course.

"See?" Jazzy said. "I told you we'd be best friends."

She gave me another hug. I hugged her back.

"But wait," I said pulling back from the hug. "Are you really staying, or was that a lie to get me to fess up?"

"That was not a lie!" Jazzy said. "I'm really staying and going to school with you and everything."

I couldn't help but laugh. "Okay, now I *am* excited. I have a best friend and the cutest shirt to wear for the first day of school. This year is going to be epic!"

My new best friend agreed.

Acknowledgments

Writing acknowledgments is hard. Writing books is hard too, and without help from others, it wouldn't happen, so bear with me while I thank a few folks.

First, to the fine people at Orca who made this book possible: Tanya Trafford, my editor, who saw something in my work and encouraged me to write this book. Thank you for welcoming me to the pod with open…er…fins? Also for laughing at my jokes, getting me, and loving Track Changes as much as I do. Thank you to Andrew Wooldridge for publishing great books from Canadian authors. We are so proud to be able to find amazing Canadian homes for our work, so thank you for that support. The kids thank you too. To the sales and marketing team—you are tireless and awesome. Thank you for ensuring this book gets into the hands of kids who will love it.

As always, a big thanks to my husband, Deke, Team Snow co-captain, head cheerleader, book-event driver and facilitator, and stalwart supporter of absolutely everything I do.

Zero thanks go out to all my pets who, while cute and entertaining, are often so disruptive that this book was written in spite of them, without any help whatsoever. Take that, jerks.

If you are only reading these acknowledgments because you expected to see your name here, well, obviously I forgot about your contribution because I have a horrible memory, but I thank you too.

Joanne Levy is the author of a number of books for young people, including *Crushing It* and *Small Medium at Large*. She lives in Ontario with her husband and kids of the furred and feathered variety.